S⚽CCER SQUAD

STARS!

Bali Rai

Illustrated by Mike Phillips

RED FOX

SOCCER SQUAD: STARS!
A RED FOX BOOK 978 1 862 30657 8

Published in Great Britain by Red Fox,
an imprint of Random House Children's Publishers UK
A Random House Group Company

This edition published 2009

11

Set in 14/22pt Meta Normal

Red Fox Books are published by Random House Children's Publishers UK,
61–63 Uxbridge Road, London W5 5SA

www.**randomhousechildrens**.co.uk
www.randomhouse.co.uk

Addresses for companies within The Random House Group Limited can be found at:
www.randomhouse.co.uk/offices.htm

THE RANDOM HOUSE GROUP Limited Reg. No. 954009

A CIP catalogue record for this book is available from the British Library.

Penguin Random House is committed to a sustainable future for our business, our readers and our planet. This book is made from Forest Stewardship Council® certified paper.

Printed and bound in Great Britain by Clays Ltd, Elcograf S.p.A.

Abs took the ball in his stride   beat his defender. He was one on on   ith their goalie.

'SHOOT!' I heard our coaches shout at the same time.

But Abs didn't shoot. Instead he tried to run the ball into the net by taking on their goal-keeper. That gave Mo all the time he needed and he robbed the ball off Abs's toe and cleared it. The ball ran out for a throw-in.

'*Idiot!*' I shouted.

The ref ran over and told me to watch my language.

'Sorry, sir,' I said.

'No more of that, son,' he warned.

Abs trotted up to me and shrugged. 'I'm gonna do him next time,' he boasted. 'Just watch. Those TV people are going to love me!'

Read every book in this action-packed

football series:

STARTING ELEVEN

MISSING!

STARS!

Coming soon:

GLORY!

STARS!

Chapter 1

Saturday

'On my head, Chris!'

I looked up and saw my best mate, Dal, running into the opposition penalty area. I had two defenders in my way. I pushed the ball to the left and then flicked it to the right, leaving the opposition players for dead. With the outside of my left foot I crossed the ball towards Dal. But it didn't go where I meant it to. Instead it sailed behind the goalie and curled into the back of the net. The crowd, all eighty thousand of them, roared! I'd won the Champions League for my team. Liverpool FC were Kings of Europe!

'CHRIS!!!!!!!!!!!!!!!!!!!!!!!!'

I shook my head and opened my eyes. I'd been dreaming. Instead of being at Wembley, playing in the Champions League final, I was at home, in bed. I groaned.

'WAKE UP!' shouted my mum.

'Coming,' I mumbled. 'Just five more minutes . . .'

Half an hour later I was sitting at the kitchen table eating my breakfast.

'Do you want some more?' my mum asked.

I looked down at the porridge in my bowl, all lumpy and tasteless and grey. I shook my head.

'I'll have a banana,' I said.

'Make sure you do, and hurry up! You have to be at football in an hour.'

My real football team was called Rushton Reds and we played in the local junior league. All three of my best friends, Dal, Abs and Jason, played too. And then there were the *girls* – the Football Barbies. Our team was the only one in the league with girls playing for it and it was kind of embarrassing. The other teams laughed at us and thought we were rubbish. To begin with, we were too. But we'd finally won our first game and now things were on the up. I couldn't wait to play against Streetly Celtic, our next opponents.

I play as a striker alongside Abs. Jason plays in midfield and my best friend since I was little, Dal, plays in defence. We're all pretty good, but then so are the girls, to be honest. Especially Lily, who can do lots of tricks with the ball. I don't mind about the girls playing any more. I've got used to them now, but Abs is always moaning about them and I knew that he would be doing it again when I got to the game.

'Hurry up, Chris!' said Mum.

'I'm finished,' I replied, smiling.

My mum drove me to Streetly Celtic's ground, which is on the far side of town. Along the way we picked up Dal, who was also running late, and his mum too.

'Hi, Mrs Singh,' I said.

'Morning, Chris – how are you?' replied Dal's mum.

'I'm OK,' I said, looking at Dal. He was about the same height as me with short brown hair and he was quite big. Not like fat or anything – just broad.

'What?' he asked with a shrug.

'Huh?' I replied.

'You're looking at me,' he said.

'No I'm not,' I protested.

'Weirdo . . .'

'Idiot . . .'

'LADS!' said Mrs Singh in a stern voice.

'Sorry,' we said at exactly the same time.

Dal's mum looked at my mum and they both burst into laughter.

'The same as when they met,' said Dal's mum.

'And they'll be the same when they're fifty too!' added mine.

Then they started talking about boring 'mum stuff' and left us alone.

'Can't wait for the game,' said Dal.

'Yeah!' I replied, getting really excited.

The drive took twenty minutes and the rest of the team were there when we arrived. I almost jumped out of the car I was so eager to start playing. And Dal was right behind me. We ran into the changing rooms.

Streetly's pitch used to be a cricket ground and the changing rooms were in an old hut behind one of the goals. The rest of the lads were waiting for us, along with two of our three coaches, Steve and Ian. The third coach, Wendy, was with the girls.

'Let's keep focused today, lads,' said Ian as we started to get changed.

I said hello to some of the other lads – Byron, Ben and Corky, as well as my cousin, Leon – and they said hello back. Next to Corky, I saw one of our goalies, Gurinder. He looked sad.

'What's up with you?' I asked him.

'My ankle is still really sore,' he explained, his shoulders sagging.

The coaches had taken us paintballing two weekends earlier and Gurinder had slipped in the mud. Our reserve keeper, Gem, had taken over between the posts since then.

'Ian says that I can't play but I'm OK,' he said. 'Honest.'

I nodded because I couldn't think of any-

thing else to do. Ian must have told Gurinder
he couldn't play for a reason. It would have
been to help him get fit. I told him what I
thought, but he just shook his head.

'I think he'd just rather play another girl in
the team,' he told me. 'That's what my
brother said . . .'

'No way,' I replied. 'Gem only got in
because you hurt yourself. She's really good
but you're the first choice. It's just because
your ankle isn't healed yet.'

Gurinder shrugged and turned away.

'What's up with misery guts?' Abs asked
me.

'He can't play,' I told him.

'Nor can you,' he said, trying to make a
joke. 'But that doesn't stop you from trying!'

'That was the lamest joke in the world,
Abs. It was like *so* unfunny there are people
in Australia crying because it was so bad,'
I said.

'Just because you ain't funny,' he replied. 'Peanut-head fool . . .'

'*Peanut*-head?' I asked. 'Where'd you get that from?'

Abs grinned. He was a bit taller than me and skinny and his hair was shaved to his head. He had tramlines cut into it, three straight lines which ran around his head.

'I told you,' he said. 'I'm funny and you ain't. I got hundreds of them too.' He nodded towards Dal. 'He's a pancake-face,' he said.

'Er . . .'

'And Jason is a big pasty – with vegetables in it . . . and big ears too!' he added.

Jason has ears that stick out quite a lot and masses of freckles. He's tall too, so he looks a bit funny sometimes. But he's cool. And he definitely didn't look like a pasty.

I turned to Dal, who was listening.

'He's gone mad,' I said.

'*Gone?* He's always been like that . . .'

'Jealous,' said Abs.

'RIGHT, LADS!' shouted Ian.

We stopped messing about and turned to face him.

'We've got a tough game on today,' he continued. 'This lot have won their last two fixtures and they score plenty of goals so we need to be aware. Unfortunately Gurinder is still unfit so Gem will continue in goal . . .'

Abs, Gurinder and Ant, another one of our squad, groaned. Steve, the second coach, gave them a stern look.

'Now now, lads,' added Ian, 'there's no need for that. We are a team with girls in it – get used to it!'

Abs's face went red and he looked away. Ant looked down at his feet and Gurinder looked like he was going to start crying. I wanted to laugh but I didn't. Instead I listened carefully as Steve read out the team sheet.

'Gem in goal and a back four of Leon, Dal, Parvy and Steven. Then it's Jason, Byron, Corky and Ben, with Abs and Chris up front – OK?'

No one said anything. There was only one girl playing other than Gem – Parvy; Lily, who had been the star in the last few games, was a substitute.

'Any questions?' asked Ian.

'Yeah,' replied Corky. 'How many substitutes are there?'

Ian thought about it. 'We've got Lily, Ant, Pete, Penny and Emma,' he replied. 'There aren't any more players.'

Corky nodded. 'My sister wants to join,' he said.

Abs put his head in his hands.

Ian smiled. 'She's very welcome to come along to the next training session,' he told Corky.

'We need to get some extra players

anyway,' I added. 'What if we get more injuries?'

Abs groaned. 'Yeah – but we could try asking some lads too,' he said. 'Why is every new player an *annoying girl*?'

'Don't complain!' shouted Jason. 'You love the Barbies . . .'

'Shut up, sardine-breath!' moaned Abs.

'Sardine-breath?' asked Dal.

Steve told us to shut up. 'Let's get outside and work through some warm-ups and tactics,' he said.

It was windy and cold when we got out onto the pitch and I was glad that we were doing warm-up exercises. I love training, so I was right at the front, jogging round some cones that Wendy, our American coach, had set up. Lily and Parvy were jogging next to me. Lily is short and slim, with long blonde hair. Parvy is our tallest player, alongside Steven

and Jason. She's really athletic and very fast
at running. Her hair is black and she wears it
in plaits most of the time.

'You OK about being a substitute?' I asked
Lily.

'Of course I am,' she replied. 'It's a team
game and today the coaches are trying
something new. Besides, Ben's been a sub
since the start of the season and he
deserves a game too.'

I ran round a cone, leading the rest of the squad.

'You must be a bit disappointed,' I said to Lily.

'Not in the slightest,' she said. 'The television people are here again and I don't want to look terrible on camera, do I?'

I hadn't even noticed the TV crew. They were friends with Wendy and they were interested in the Reds because we had girls playing for us. They were going to make a documentary about us – starting with today's match. We were going to be famous!

'I had my hair done specially for today,' said Parvy.

'And I got my nails done,' added Lily.

'Hey?' I asked, getting confused. 'We're playing football – they won't even see your nails . . .'

'Oh, they will!' replied Lily. 'I'll make sure that they do . . .'

I shrugged and ran round yet another cone.

'Now where's my husband?' asked Lily, talking about Dal. She'd been teasing him ever since we'd all met and Dal went bright red every time she spoke to him. It was well funny.

'He's back there,' I told her. 'Avoiding you.'

'Avoiding me?' she said, pretending to be

upset. 'Well, that just won't do at all.'

She slowed right down and fell back along the line. I grinned at Parvy.

'She's funny,' I told her.

Parvy nodded. 'Come on,' she said. 'Last one to the next cone is a big fat donkey . . . !'

She sprinted off and left me behind.

I smiled and sprinted after her.

Chapter 2

Streetly kicked off the game and they were all over us for the first five minutes. I spent the beginning of the match helping the team to defend and didn't get anywhere close to Streetly's goal. They had some really good players – in the middle were identical twins who were called Ali and Mo.

Now Mo was running with the ball and as Jason made a challenge, he skipped to the right. Jason was left stranded. I sprinted into the space behind my team-mate and faced up to Mo. Just as he was about to make a pass I stepped in and took the ball away from him. Mo let out a growling sound, but he didn't try and win the ball back. He just stood where he was and moaned at his brother.

'You could have helped me,' I heard him shouting.

I ran through the middle of the pitch and saw Ben out on the left wing. I passed the ball to his feet, just as Ian had shown me. Then I ran into a space, at an angle to Ben, where he could pass me the ball if he wanted to. But he didn't. Instead he raced down the line and crossed the ball over to the right of Streetly's penalty area, where Abs picked it up.

I had a defender next to me and I knew that I had to get rid of him. I turned to face the goal and started to run to the left. The defender, who was about twice my height and heavy with it, followed. But I spun to the right and sprinted into a wide open space in the box.

'ABS!' I screamed.

All he had to do was roll the ball in front of me and we'd have a goal.

But he didn't do it. Instead I saw him look over at the touchline where the cameraman was holding a small handheld recorder. Then Abs took the ball and started to do tricks with it. The defender facing him went to make a tackle, but Abs rolled the ball under his foot. He spun it left and right and left again and then tried to nutmeg the defender. But he got it wrong and the defender just ran away with the ball.

'ABS!' I shouted. 'I WAS IN THE CLEAR!'

He shrugged and trotted back into position as though there was no problem. He was wrong.

As I sprinted back to try and dispossess

the defender, he passed it to Ali, who went on a twisting, jinking run into our penalty area. Everyone who tried to tackle him failed. Then Steven and Dal made a mistake. Both of them went towards Ali, which let his brother Mo move into a dangerous position.

I shouted at Parvy, who spotted the danger and left the lad she was marking. But even though she was quick, Ali was quicker. As Steven and Dal closed in, he simply passed the ball into the space they'd left. Mo ran onto the ball and smashed it, just as Parvy flew in. The ball deflected off Parvy's knee and sent Gem the wrong way.

It was 1–0 to Streetly!

'NAH!!!!!!!!!!!!!!!!!' I groaned.

As I trudged slowly back to the centre, one of the Streetly team wound me up.

'We're gonna score five!' he told me.

'In your dreams,' I told him.

'What you gonna do – get a girl to win the game for you?' he added.

I looked over at the touchline where Lily and Penny were talking to the woman who was making the programme.

'We'll win,' I told the lad. 'Just watch . . .'

He laughed at me and walked off.

From the restart Streetly were on the attack again and I could hear our coaches screaming at us from the sidelines. They were right too. We weren't playing like a team. We had no shape and every time we got the ball, instead of passing it to each other, we were losing it.

And Abs was on another planet. I played him in behind the defender twice in the next ten minutes. Each time, instead of passing the ball into space for me or another player to run onto, he stopped and started to do fancy tricks. But he kept getting them wrong and losing the ball. I was getting really angry with him. It was like he was trying to be a star instead of playing for the team.

Finally we managed to get hold of the ball and keep it for a while. Parvy started a really good move by turning her opponent inside out and then going on a run down the left. She skipped past two Streetly players and turned inside. Looking up, she squared the ball to Jason, who took it on. He beat his marker and played Corky in.

Corky ran for the box and got to the touchline, where he crossed the ball along the ground. Ben, who had come in from his position on the wing, received the ball with his back to goal. There were two defenders behind him, and instead of trying to take them on he passed the ball to me.

I tried to turn inside my marker but there was no space. Ali was snapping at my heels and I didn't know what to do. Suddenly Abs ran across me and told me to lay the ball off to him. I hesitated for a split second before passing.

Abs took the ball in his stride and beat his defender. He was one on one with their goalie.

'SHOOT!' I heard our coaches shout at the same time.

But Abs didn't shoot. Instead he tried to run the ball into the net by taking on their goalkeeper. That gave Mo all the time he needed and he robbed the ball off Abs's toe and cleared it. The ball ran out for a throw-in.

'*Idiot!*' I shouted.

The ref ran over and told me to watch my language.

'Sorry, sir,' I said.

'No more of that, son,' he warned.

Abs trotted up to me and shrugged.

'I'm gonna do him next time,' he boasted.

'Just watch. Those TV people are going to love me!'

I wanted to say something but I didn't. Instead I walked off and stood with Jason, waiting for the game to begin again.

'He's showing off for the camera,' Jason said.

'I know,' I replied. 'And it's not fair. We should be winning by now . . .'

Jason nodded in agreement as Corky took the throw-in. The ball fell to Abs and, with the defender right behind him, all he had to do was pass to Parvy, who was free.

But Abs tried to back-heel the ball and nutmeg his defender. The ball bounced off the defender's shin pads and went straight to Mo, who set off on another run. This time he passed to Streetly's right winger. The winger was short and skilful and he turned Leon inside out. Leon stumbled and went down holding his ankle. The winger crossed for Ali, who controlled the ball and beat Gem at the near post.

2–0!

This time I didn't moan. Instead I got the ball and ran back to the centre circle with it. We had five minutes left in the first half and I was determined that we would get at least one goal back. From the start I ignored Abs and passed to Ben. He ran down the left wing, with me and Byron close by. Ben passed to Byron, who didn't waste any time. He passed the ball straight on to me. By this point Ben was in more space and I took one touch and then played Ben in behind his defender.

I turned and ran for the goal. Ben took on his man and then found Byron, who ran for the touchline.

Two Streetly defenders went to him and I was free. Byron saw me and squared the ball. It trickled slowly along the goal line, beating the goalkeeper and the defenders.

Everything slowed right down. The ball was right there in front of me, on the goal line. All I had to do was tap it home. But just as I lunged for the ball I felt myself being tugged back. It was Abs! As he pulled on my shirt I tried in vain to reach the ball.

'Leave it – it's mine!' Abs shouted. He kicked out his foot and made contact with the ball. But instead of scoring, he somehow

managed to scoop the ball up and away, just past the left-hand post.

The Streetly players began to laugh.

'You'd better get those girls on the pitch,' Mo said to me as he ran past.

Abs held up his hands. 'I'm sorry,' he said. 'I just wanted to score.'

I shrugged and walked away. He just wanted to look good in front of the television crew!

Two minutes later we did score though.
Parvy started another move and this time
Byron made no mistake. He played a one-
two with me and then smashed the ball past
the Streetly keeper.

2–1!

No one on our team celebrated the goal.
Instead Jason picked up the ball and ran
back to the centre circle. We were back in
the game: now we had to score at least two
more goals to win!

At half-time Wendy and Ian told us that
Steve had gone home.

'He said he couldn't stay and watch this
nonsense,' Wendy told us. 'And he was right
too. You are all so much better than that.
What's going on out there?'

Everyone spoke at once.

'OK! OK!' said Wendy. 'Just get out there
and change things around. Pass the ball to

each other – the simple pass – and move into good spaces. Little triangles . . .'

Ian cleared his throat. 'We're making two substitutions before the restart,' he told us. 'Emma is coming on for Leon – he'd better rest that ankle a bit – and Lily is replacing Abs.'

'NAH!' shouted Abs. 'That's not fair . . .'

Ian shook his head. 'You don't question,' he told Abs. 'This is for the good of the team. You've had the first half, Abs, and now it's Lily's turn . . .'

I put up my hand.

'Yes, Chris?' asked Wendy.

'Who's going to play up front with me then?' I asked.

'I am,' replied Lily, beaming a smile in my direction.

'Oh,' I said.

Lily was a winger and I wasn't sure she could play as a striker. But then again she

would at least *pass* the ball. She turned
to Dal.

'Now, husband dearest, just get the ball
to me and I'll set up Chris for the goals . . . is
that clear?'

Dal looked confused. He wasn't sure if Lily
was joking or not and I wasn't either. But
after her last game I wasn't going to
question her. She was a good player.

'Football ninjas to the rescue,' she
declared. The rest of the girls laughed.

'What does that mean?' I asked.

Parvy shook her head. 'It's not a boy
thing,' she told me. 'It's for girls only . . .'

'Come on, REDS!' shouted Wendy. 'Let's
kick some butt!'

And that's exactly what we did. We ended up
winning 3–2. Byron scored the second and I
scored the winner. Lily set both of them up,
backed up by Ben and Emma, who played

really well together on the right. As we walked off the pitch at the end, joking and laughing, I saw Abs mooching about. He looked really unhappy.

'You OK, Abs?' I asked.

'No!' he snapped like a five-year-old. 'Ain't fair – that's my position, not hers!'

I was going to say something, but he didn't wait for me. Instead he walked off in a strop.

Chapter 3

Tuesday

When I walked into the youth club where we play, everyone was already there. I saw Abs standing talking with Gurinder and Ant.

'Smells in here,' I said to him.

Abs shrugged. 'Maybe,' he said.

I gave him a funny look. Was there something up with him? 'You OK?' I asked.

He nodded and then continued his conversation with the other two. Wondering if I'd done something wrong, I turned to Lily and Penny, who were standing close by.

'Do *you* think it smells?' I asked them.

'Yes,' replied Penny. 'Too many *boys* . . .'

I grinned. 'I'm being serious,' I told her. I was too. There was a really strange smell in the youth club – like bleach mixed with flowers. And it was really strong. My nose was itching and my eyes were beginning to sting.

'Now that you come to mention it,' said Lily, 'it does pong a bit.'

'Told you.'

'I'm going to find Wendy,' replied Lily.

She walked off towards the corridor which led to some offices and down to the changing rooms. But she didn't get very far. As she reached the door, it opened, and Wendy came through with the people from the TV station.

'Hey!' Wendy said to everyone. 'The TV crew are here . . . *Oh, my God* – what's that smell?'

'I was just coming to tell you, Wendy,' Lily told her.

'It's awful!' said Wendy.

'My eyes are stinging,' I complained.

Wendy said something to the TV people and then she turned to us.

'I think there's been some sort of accident with bleach in here. Whatever it is, I think we need to go and stand outside . . .'

She went over to the door and propped it open.

'OK, REDS – LET'S GO!' she shouted.

Lily and Penny led the way as we trudged outside where the wind was strong and cold.

'It's freezing out here!' said Dal, who had suddenly appeared at my side like a ghost. Jason was next to him.

'Where did you come from?' I asked him.

'Just there,' he said, without showing me where he meant.

'Oh, there you are, my darling husband,'

Lily said to Dal, teasing him like she always did.

'Don't say that!' complained Dal.

'Why not?' said Lily with a smile.

'Because I'm not your husband, am I?' Dal reminded her.

Lily's face fell. Her bottom lip began to quiver. I looked at Dal. His face started to go red. He'd obviously really upset Lily and I could tell that he was starting to feel bad about it.

'I . . . I . . .' he stuttered.

'GOTCHA!' laughed Lily and Penny started to giggle.

'That's not fair!' said Dal as me and Jason started laughing at him too.

'Oh, do be quiet,' replied Lily. 'You sound like Abs . . .'

We walked over to the edge of the football pitch, where Wendy was talking to the TV people. The rest of the team were standing around chatting.

'What are we doing today?' Penny asked Wendy.

Wendy gave her a big smile. 'OK, Reds,' she said to all of us. 'Gather round.'

The whole squad stopped what they were doing and listened.

'Today we are going to have a slightly different training session. Ian and Steve aren't here so I'll be running it. I'd also like to introduce you all to Hayley, Brian and John.'

The three people from the TV station said hello.

'Are you going to make us famous?' asked Byron.

'Er . . . maybe,' replied Hayley.

She was about the same height as Wendy, with curly brown hair.

'Do you think we'll be talent-spotted by the Premiership?' said Abs.

'Who knows?' Hayley told him. 'Anything is possible.'

'Never mind about all of that,' Wendy added. 'Let's just get on with the training session. Go and get changed and I'll see you all out here in ten minutes.'

'But what about the nasty smell?' asked Penny.

'If all the girls go home, it'll stop,' replied Gurinder meanly.

Some of the lads started to laugh. Abs and Ant joined in. The girls looked angry. Wendy held up her hand and told them to stop.

'It's very simple,' she told us. 'As you all know, Rushton Reds is a special team and anyone who doesn't want to be a part of it is welcome to leave.'

I looked at the faces of my team-mates.

Everyone looked shocked. Wendy was normally really cheerful. She must have been really upset at what Gurinder had said. Her voice had been very stern.

'No?' she added when no one spoke up. 'Good. Now go and get changed. I've checked the changing rooms and they are OK. The problem is with the clubroom.'

As we walked into the changing rooms, I asked Dal and Jason if they thought that Abs was acting strangely.

'Yeah,' Dal told me. 'He hasn't even spoken to me.'

'Wonder what's up with him?' I added.

'Dunno,' said Jason, 'but he isn't even hanging out with us.'

I decided to see how Abs acted during the training session. We were normally paired together and if there was something wrong, I'd find out.

Chapter 4

Wendy split us into two groups and told us that we'd be practising set plays. She explained that we needed to work on free kicks, corners and shooting. She sent my group to the goal at the far end from where we were standing. Abs and Gurinder were in the same group as me, and as we made our way to the other end, I asked Abs if he was OK.

'Suppose,' he replied before turning to start a conversation with Gurinder.

Jason, who was also in my group, saw what Abs did and came up to me.

'There *is* something wrong with him, Chris, isn't there?' he asked.

I nodded. 'Don't know what, though,' I replied. 'I haven't said anything to him.'

As we started to kick some balls around, Wendy walked over and split our group into two again.

'Chris's team are going to attack,' she told us. 'And Abs's team will defend. And after five plays, you'll switch. Is that clear?'

'What are plays?' asked Byron, who was with us too.

'Five *attempts*, silly,' explained Parvy. 'We get to try five corners first, and then Abs's team do the same.'

'Oh,' said Byron. 'That's easy . . .'

'We'll see,' said Wendy.

She told us that she wanted us to think about where we stood when a corner kick was taken. The attacking team needed to look for spaces and the defenders needed to make sure that there weren't any.

'And let's try and get the ball right into the box from the kick,' she added. 'I know it's quite far to kick the ball, but with practice it'll get easier.'

I nodded as she explained a bit more and then smiled when she mentioned that we'd be practising penalties too. I loved taking penalties. I had never missed one. Not ever. But I hadn't taken a single penalty for the Reds and I was hoping that when Wendy saw how good I was at them, she'd make me the team's first-choice penalty-taker.

'OK, people – let's get to it!' she shouted. 'Oh, and please try and ignore Hayley and her crew. They will just be watching for now, but later on you'll get the chance to speak to them so you can all try and be stars then. Right now I want to see you working hard on these plays – got it?'

'Yes, Wendy,' a few of us said.

We didn't score a single goal during the corner practice, and nor did Abs's team. But when we got to the free kicks, my team scored twice.

Abs had a face like thunder when his attempt missed, and when I said, 'Better luck next time,' he just scowled at me and walked away. Then Parvy scored with her free kick too and Abs started to moan. But I was used to him moaning so I ignored him.

We practised some more plays and then Wendy came back over and told us to start a penalty shoot-out.

Abs's team had the first penalty. I had to decide who would go in goal for us. My mini-team was me, Parvy, Jason and Byron.

'I'll go in,' I told them, pulling on the goalie gloves.

'Good,' replied Parvy. 'I hate playing in goal. Goalkeepers are weird . . .'

'What's weird about goalkeepers?' I asked her.

'Dunno,' she said. 'They're just weird . . .'

Abs had Gurinder, Emma and Corky on his side and Corky was the first to take a shot at goal. I bounced up and down on the line like proper goalkeepers do on the telly, and when Corky took his shot I dived to my left. But the ball went the other way and they led 1–0.

'EASY!' shouted Abs and Gurinder together.

I walked back to my team and let Gurinder go in goal. Byron got a football and set it down on the penalty spot. He turned and took five steps, winked at us, and then spun round to face the ball. Gurinder was moving along the line, from side to side, and pulling really strange faces – like people do when

they've eaten too much. When Byron kicked the ball, Gurinder went the right way, but Byron's shot was too strong. It flew past the goalie and into the net.

1–1.

'Who's scoring easy now then?' shouted Jason, getting excited.

'You lot are rubbish!' shouted Gurinder as I took up my position in goal. This time it was Emma's turn to take a penalty. And this time I guessed the right way and saved her shot. I ran back to my team – happy that I'd saved a goal.

'OH NO!' groaned Abs. 'I *knew* we shouldn't have let *her* take it! She's a *girl* . . .' He and Gurinder smirked together.

Parvy looked at me. 'Your friend is really, really, really horrible,' she said.

'He's only messing about,' I replied, trying to defend Abs.

'He's just made Emma *cry*,' Jason said.

I looked over and saw that Jason was right. And Abs was still moaning about her missing her penalty too. I walked over and told Emma that missing the shot was no big deal. Then I turned to Abs.

'You aren't being fair,' I told him.

'So?' he asked.

'You have to say sorry to Emma.'

'No,' he replied, acting like a five-year-old.

Emma told me that she was OK now anyway and walked over to Parvy and the others. Corky went with her. Abs went and got the ball.

'Your go next, Chris,' he told me.

I looked at Jason and Parvy. I didn't want to take my turn.

'I'm not playing,' I told Abs.

'But you have to,' he replied. 'Wendy will tell you off.'

'No she won't,' I told him.

I walked over to the others and left Abs

standing with Gurinder. If he was going to be so silly, I didn't want to play with him.

Emma and the rest of the girls were part of the team. They were part of Rushton Reds. You weren't supposed to pick on your own team-mates. And without the girls, where would our team be?

Chapter 5

Wendy took Abs and Gurinder to one side after we'd told her what had happened. I watched from a distance as Abs pulled his 'being told off' face. I felt bad that I'd sided against him, but then Dal told me that I had done the right thing.

'He's the one who's being silly, Chris,' he said.

'I know, but he's still our friend . . .' I replied.

'Doesn't act like it,' added Jason. 'I can't

believe how he's going on. He's like a baby.'

I looked over again and saw that Abs was really angry. He said something to Wendy and walked off. Wendy turned round and walked over to us.

'OK, Reds – let's get on with the session,' she said.

'Where's Abs going?' asked Lily.

'He's going to cool off,' Wendy replied. 'Nothing serious. Now let's get some shooting practice set up!'

The TV people watched us as we took turns to shoot at Gem in one of the goals. We were standing in a line, facing the goal, and Wendy was to our right, halfway between the first person in line and the goal. Each time she blew on her whistle, the first person ran forward and Wendy passed them the ball. They took a maximum of three touches and then shot at goal.

Gem was great. She saved the first three

shots, and when I took mine, she tipped it over the bar. It was like watching a real proper Premiership keeper, only Gem was much smaller and a girl.

The first person to score was Lily. She lifted the ball up over Gem's head and it sailed in. The rest of us clapped as Lily pretended to do a silly celebration dance. She stood and moved her arms up and down in a jerking motion, pretending that she was a robot. It was well funny.

Wendy made us run through the exercise three more times. Then she told half of us to go and talk to the TV crew.

Lily, Jason, Dal, Parvy, Emma, Byron, Ben and Leon followed me over to where Hayley was standing. Brian was holding the camera, which was really small, and John was looking at his clipboard.

'OK, kids!' Hayley said cheerfully. 'We're going to do a little question and answer session, OK?'

We all nodded.

'Now,' she continued, 'I'm going to ask you some questions and I want you to tell me your thoughts. Don't all speak at once, please. If you have something you want to say, put up your hand and I'll get round to you. Is that clear?'

'YESSS!' we all replied.

'Will this be on the television tonight?' asked Ben.

'Don't be silly,' Emma told him. 'They haven't even made the show yet.'

'I was only asking,' moaned Ben. He looked a bit upset.

'I'm sorry,' replied Emma. She punched him on the arm.

''S OK,' Ben told her, smiling as he did so.

Hayley told us to stand in a semi-circle and then she asked Brian to come over and start filming us. John, who was still looking at his clipboard, asked us to call out our names so that he could tick them off.

'BEN!' 'BYRON!' 'EMMA!' 'LEON!' 'DAL!' 'LILY!' 'JASON!' 'CHRIS!' 'PARVY!' we all said in turn.

'OK – now I'm going to ask the first question,' Hayley told us. 'Try and act naturally and forget that there is a camera filming you. Look at me when you reply rather than over at Brian . . .'

'Are we going to be famous, miss?' asked Leon.

'Just do as I say,' replied Hayley. She smiled, but it was one of those smiles like my mum does sometimes. Underneath she's getting wound up but she tries not to show it. Usually when I've done something wrong, which is, like, most of the time!

'OK . . . what do you all honestly think of playing in a mixed team?' Hayley asked.

Everyone put up their hands and Hayley

picked Dal to answer first.

'I didn't like it to begin with,' he told her. 'I thought the Reds were a boys' team . . .'

Lily was pushing her hand into the air excitedly. She was trying really hard to get Hayley's attention.

Dal carried on. 'We thought that they would be . . . er . . . not . . . er . . . very good and that,' he added.

'And are they good?' asked Hayley, with a proper smile this time.

Dal nodded.

'And girls – what do you think of—?' began Hayley, only for Lily to cut in.

'Well I think we've been a *great* success,' she said as she straightened her hair and looked directly into the camera. 'I mean – it's been *difficult* having to put up with the name-calling and the rudeness, but we've done very well. And tactically we are better than them, except for *Dal,* who is really clever and the best footballer by miles in the team and . . . and . . . and Wendy is a woman and *she's* a coach, which is really, really, really great, don't you think?'

'Oh—' began Hayley.

Lily didn't let her get another word in. 'We train the same as the boys,' she added hurriedly. 'And we're better at lots of stuff and I think that without us the Reds wouldn't be half as good and . . . and . . . and . . .'

'Take a breath,' Hayley told her.

Lily straightened more of her hair and smiled. 'I'm OK,' she told Hayley. 'Now where was I? Oh, *yes* – the *boys*. Well, most of them have been really nice after complaining at the beginning. They really love us now and it's all because we—'

'She's a right chatterbox!' laughed Byron, interrupting.

'I'm just trying to get my point across,' complained Lily.

Hayley put on my mum's smile again and turned to me.

'Let's see what someone else has to say,' she told us. 'So, are you totally happy with the girls, Chris?' she asked me.

I shrugged. 'They're *OK*,' I told her. 'Lily has won us a couple of games with her goals and they can tackle and everything. I didn't think they'd be able to play against really good boy players but they can. It's like it doesn't matter if we're stronger than them . . .'

'*You are not stronger!*' shouted Parvy.

I looked at the cameraman.

'Over here please, Chris,' said Hayley.

I nodded. 'I didn't mean it like that,' I told Parvy. 'I don't mean that we're . . . Well, I do mean it, but not in the way that you think and–'

Parvy snorted. 'I could kick your butt any day of the week,' she told me. 'Shooting, running, training – anything you want.'

'But I only meant that some of the lads we play against are quite big,' I added.

'Big like empty barrels,' Lily told me. 'And empty barrels make the most noise when you break them . . . my dad told me that.'

Hayley held up her hands. 'OK, OK . . .' she told us. 'Try not to get too carried away. Now who thinks that Rushton Reds can actually win the league or the Cup?'

Every single one of us shouted out: 'Me!' 'Me!' 'Me!'

'Even against teams which have all-male squads?' she added.

'YES!' shouted Parvy.

'But you started the season very slowly . . .'

'And now we're getting better,' replied Byron and Dal together.

Jason nodded and joined in. 'We're going really well,' he told Hayley. 'We really play as a team and the coaches are brilliant.'

'So, glory for the Reds then?' asked Hayley.

'WE ARE THE REDS! WE ARE THE REDS! WE ARE THE REDS!' Byron sang out.

The rest of us looked at each other and started to laugh.

'What you laughing at?' asked Byron.

'We're laughing at you, you silly sausage!' Lily replied.

Hayley asked us a few more questions and then we went back to shooting practice as the other half of the squad had their turn in front of the camera.

Abs had gone home by the time we finished practice, which meant that I didn't have a lift. I told Wendy that I was stuck. Abs should have told me he was going but he didn't. It was as though he had fallen out with all of us and didn't care any more. I didn't like it.

'I'll take you,' Wendy said. 'Just use my phone and call your parents to ask them if that's OK.'

She handed me a pink phone. It was tiny but I still felt silly holding it. It was pink! And it had flowers printed on it. YUK! After I'd called my mum, Wendy asked me why I hadn't gone with Dal or Jason.

'Dal's dad is taking him into town and Jason went to go see his nan,' I explained.

'OK. And what did you think of the TV crew?' she added.

''S OK,' I replied. 'What did Abs say to you?'

Wendy shrugged as she led me out to her car. 'Oh, nothing much,' she said, but I could tell that she was hiding something.

'Did he quit?' I asked.

'Quit? Oh, no – I just told him to go and cool off. He'll be back for the next training session.'

I nodded.

'Although he will have to start being nicer to the girls . . .'

I nodded again. 'I think he'll be OK,' I told her.

'Let's hope so – he's a very fine attacker,' she said. 'Even if he is a little bit greedy on the ball!'

I grinned. 'He's like that all the time,' I said. 'Will Ian and Steve be back for the next session?'

'Er . . . Ian will,' she said. 'Steve is a bit . . . er . . . busy with his family.'

I didn't ask any more questions after that. Instead, as Wendy drove me home, I wondered whether Abs would be OK with me at school the following day. I hoped so. Abs could be a bit stupid sometimes, but he was cool too.

And he was one of my best friends.

Chapter 6

Wednesday

'Ain't talking to you!' Abs told me as I sat on the wall outside our classroom the next morning.

'*Hey!* Why aren't you talking to me?' I asked.

'Because I'm not!' he replied.

'What about me?' asked Dal, who was standing beside me.

'None of you. We aren't friends any more . . .' Abs told us.

He walked off into the classroom as Jason came up.

'What's wrong with Abs?' he asked.

'I don't know,' I told him. 'He said he isn't our friend any more.'

'Why?' Jason looked really upset.

I shrugged.

'I bet it's got to do with what happened yesterday at football,' said Dal.

'He was really strange then too,' I added. 'He only spoke to Gurinder and Ant.'

Dal asked me what we were going to do.

'We haven't done anything wrong,' I told him. 'Abs is the one who's being a baby.'

'Yeah, Chris, but he's our friend,' said Jason.

I shook my head. 'You didn't hear him,' I replied. 'He said he doesn't want to be our friend.'

For the rest of the morning Abs didn't even look at me, Dal or Jason, even though we're all in the same class. We were doing a project on recycling and I was trying to draw a picture of a paper-recycling machine. Abs was supposed to help me with it. But he stayed on the other side of the classroom, talking to a lad called Dylan. When the teacher, Miss Chohan, asked him why he wasn't working with me, he just shrugged and said that he'd changed partners to be with Dylan.

'I told him I was going to change,' Abs told Miss Chohan.

But he was lying. He hadn't told me. I wanted to say something, but before I could Lily and Parvy walked into our classroom.

'Hello!' Parvy said, smiling at me like those crazy old people on the bus do sometimes.

'Why are you here?' I asked.

'We're doing the project too!' she replied as Lily went over to Dal and gave him a hug. She's always doing that – pretending that they're going out with each other. Dal gets

63

really embarrassed by it.

'Don't do that!' he complained as two lads from our class, Nilesh and Mark, started to giggle like little five-year-old girls.

'What you laughing at?' Dal asked them. He was getting upset.

'Your big ugly face!' Nilesh told him.

Lily spun round to face Nilesh and put her hands on her hips.

'Don't you dare call my husband ugly!' she told him. 'I'd tell you to look in a mirror but you broke them all so you can't,' she added.

'EHH!!!! Nilesh got beat by a girl!' shouted another lad, Paulo, just as Lily turned back and Nilesh leaned forward and pinched her – hard – then tugged at her hair.

Miss Chohan looked up. 'Who's beating who?' she asked.

'No one, miss,' Lily told her. 'It was just Nilesh. He pulled my hair, but I'm OK . . .'

'NILESH PATEL!' shouted Miss Chohan.

'But I never, miss – I never!' protested Nilesh.

Only Miss Chohan didn't believe him. She marched over and told Nilesh to go and see Mr Williams, the school deputy head.

'You don't pull hair,' she told him.

'But he didn't do it, miss,' came a shout from behind us. It was Abs. 'Lily is lying. It was Chris who done it!'

Me, Dal, Jason, Lily and Parvy all spun round to look at him. He shrugged at us and then grinned. But none of us grinned back. It was one thing not talking to us – but to get us in trouble with the teacher? That was just wrong.

'Lily?' asked Miss Chohan, looking concerned.

Lily let her face drop and then her lower lip began to quiver, as though she was going to cry. I knew she was faking, but the teacher didn't. She fell for it.

'Now now, Lily – no need to cry – there's a good girl,' said Miss Chohan.

'He did do it, miss,' said Lily. 'He pulled my hair and he pinched me and he told me that I was a silly poo–'

'No I didn't!' shouted Nilesh.

'ENOUGH!' shouted someone from the doorway. It was Mr Kilminster, our form teacher. He was red-faced and his eyes looked like they were going to pop out of his head. But then again he always looked like that. I felt a joke coming on.

'Do you think that's how he asks for his breakfast in the morning – by shouting at his wife?' I whispered to the others.

'Probably,' replied Parvy with a grin.

'*GET ME MY TEA!*' said Dal in a loud whisper.

'Imagine being his kids,' I added. 'That would be horrible.'

'He hasn't got kids,' whispered Lily. 'He's

far too ugly to be allowed to have them . . .'

We all started to giggle and Mr Kilminster went mad again.

'THIS IS A CLASSROOM – NOT A ZOO!' he yelled.

'Then why are *you* here?' whispered Parvy, really faintly.

This time we had to hold our laughter in. By the time we had settled down again, I'd totally forgotten Abs's betrayal. But Dal and Lily hadn't.

'Don't know what his problem is,' Lily said after about ten minutes.

'Who?' asked Jason. 'Mr Kilminster?'

'No – not him,' Dal replied. 'Abs . . .'

I grinned. Dal and Lily were thinking the same way now.

'They *must* be married,' I said to Parvy and Jason, talking about Dal and Lily. 'That's what my mum and dad do. Like, my mum will start saying something and halfway through my dad will walk into the room and finish what she's saying. It's spooky.'

'Like your sister's haircut?' asked Jason.

'No – that's SCARY,' I joked.

We laughed a bit more but soon shut up when Mr Kilminster walked towards us.

'Abs is soooo out of order,' continued Lily, in a whisper.

'It's all about football,' I replied.

'ARE YOU WORKING OR TALKING, CHRISTOPHER?'

'Working, sir,' I said.

'GOOD!' Mr Kilminster bellowed.

We waited five minutes and then Lily started whispering again.

'I think he hates me,' she said, talking about Abs.

'No, he doesn't,' Dal told her, taking the words right out of my mouth.

'Then why is he so mean?' she asked.

'I dunno,' I replied. 'I think he's just being

funny about you girls playing for the team.'

Parvy groaned. 'Is he still on about that?' she asked. 'It's been ages since then. He's just a big baby.'

Lily nodded in agreement. 'We aren't going anywhere,' she told us. 'Rushton Reds is as much our team as it is yours.'

'We know that,' said Dal.

'Why, thank you for the support, darling,' teased Lily.

'Stop it!' Dal demanded.

'Oh, don't be like that. I was only—' she began just as a familiar shout went up.

'WORK, NOT PLAY!' yelled Mr Kilminster.

That evening Dal came over for tea and we spoke more about Abs. I wanted to go round to Abs's house or call him on the phone but Dal told me to forget it.

'It won't last long,' he told me.

'What if he really does stop being our

friend – like permanently?' I asked.

'He won't,' said Dal. 'Come on – let's go on your computer. I want to check out that new Audi supercar!'

We ran upstairs and I turned on my PC so that we could surf the net. Within thirty seconds Dal had found the car he was on about. He sat and talked about how fast it went and how many valves it had, but I wasn't listening. I don't mind cars – they look great, some of them. But I don't like talking about them.

After about ten minutes, I navigated to the Liverpool FC website and we looked at that. There was loads of news on it and we down-loaded LFC screensavers too. Just as the last screensaver was loading, I noticed a small box pop up at the bottom right of the screen. It was Abs and he was signing into Messenger. I clicked on the box and the screen changed.

'He's online,' I told Dal.

'So?' asked Dal. 'If he didn't talk to us at school, he isn't going to do it online, is he?'

I shrugged. 'He might,' I replied.

I typed a quick message to him and pressed the 'send' button. The message said: 'Hello.' I waited for about five minutes and when Abs didn't reply, I sent another message which read: 'What's up, bro?' He didn't reply to that either.

'Told you,' said Dal.

I thought hard about how I could get Abs to reply. What would wind him up so much that he wouldn't be able to resist replying? I asked Dal.

'Manchester United,' he said straight away.

'Good one!' I shouted, wishing that I'd thought of it myself.

I waited a moment and then typed 'Man U are rubbish!' I pressed 'Send'.

For a minute Abs did nothing, but then 'Abs is writing a reply' flashed up.

I smiled at Dal. 'See?' I told him. 'Now we can chat to him and find out what's wrong.'

But the reply said only one thing:
'GET LOST!'

Chapter 7

Thursday

Wendy told us about Steve at Thursday's training session. He had gone home early during our last game and hadn't turned up for Tuesday's session either. I remembered Wendy telling me that he had some family problems, but she hadn't been telling me the truth. Not that she was lying or being sly or anything. She just hadn't wanted to upset me. But now she was telling us all.

'I'm afraid that Steve had a heart attack on Monday morning after feeling very ill during Saturday's game. He's in hospital, recovering, and although he's OK, he is very, very poorly.'

Ian, who looked really tired and upset, turned to us. 'I've been visiting him every day and I have to say he's fighting to get better.'

Everyone in the squad just looked at each other. I put my hand up.

'Yes, Chris?' asked Wendy.

'Will he get better?' I asked. Dal and Byron nodded as though I'd asked what they were thinking too.

'We hope so,' she replied.

'The doctors say that he's on the mend,' added Ian. 'And Steve also told me to pass on a message. He said that although you're not quite there, he feels that this team will very soon be the best junior team he has ever worked with . . .'

Hayley and the TV crew were filming us as

we stood in silence. She looked very serious, and when the rest of the squad went to get changed, she asked me and Parvy to stay behind.

'Would you like to tell me how you are feeling?' she asked us. 'For the programme?'

I nodded. John had the little camera and he pointed it at us and then said 'Go'. Hayley asked us how we felt about Steve.

'It's a big shock,' Parvy told her. 'He's really lovely and he is a great coach.'

'Yeah,' I added. 'He just wants what's best for all of us and I hope he's back soon.'

Hayley coughed a little. 'Do you think that Steve's illness will make you closer as a team?' she asked.

Parvy nodded. 'We're already quite close but yes, this should help too,' she replied.

'It's like, if we go and play on Saturday,' I said, 'we'll be thinking about him and what he always tells us to do. I know I will . . .'

Hayley smiled at us. 'So Rushton Reds to win the next game for their poorly coach?' she asked.

'Every game!' said Parvy.

'We want to win our league,' I added. 'And the Cup too . . .'

'OK,' replied Hayley. 'Thanks, kids.'

Abs, Gurinder and Ant stuck together at training again. By the time we were ready for a game, I was really upset. I'd tried to talk to Abs at least five times and he was just ignoring me. In the end Dal told me to forget about it.

'He just doesn't care,' he said.

'But I want to know what we've done wrong,' I replied.

Abs was just being weird. I couldn't think of a single reason why he wasn't talking to us. I mean, even if he was upset about the girls playing, why was he ignoring me, Dal and Jason? We were supposed to be his best mates.

When the two teams got picked for the practice match, Abs and his new friends were on the same side, and me, Jason and Dal were together. We also had Lily, Parvy and Byron with us, as well as Gem, Ben and Pete. Because there were only seventeen squad members, our team had the extra person. Abs didn't like it.

'That ain't fair!' he complained.

'Oh yes it is,' Ian told him. 'Last week you were on the team with the extra player. Just get on with it, son.'

Abs pulled a face and then said something to Ant. They both started laughing.

I turned to Dal and Jason. 'They're talking about us,' I told them.

'So what?' replied Jason. 'Let them.'

Ian and Wendy sorted out our positions and the practice match kicked off. Abs got hold of the ball straight away and went on a run right at the heart of our team. He ran past Lily and me, but when he got to Byron he lost control of the ball. Byron took it and passed it to me. I held it, with my back to goal, and then, as Lily made a move to my left, I played it into her path. It was exactly the sort of game that Steve had been trying to teach us. Quick, simple passes followed by movement off the ball. No long, hopeful balls or punts into the air.

'If God had wanted us to play soccer in the air, he'd have put grass up there,' Wendy had reminded us before the practice game. She'd stolen the saying from some old football manager that none of us had ever heard of.

Lily ran onto my pass and was through on goal. She had the perfect opportunity to score, but she didn't take it. Instead she saw that I had run into space and was totally free.

With just the keeper, Gurinder, to beat, she squared the ball to me and I simply tapped it into an empty net. I wheeled around to celebrate and saw Gurinder slide in and foul Lily. They ended up in a heap on the ground.

'*Oi!*' shouted Byron and Jason, running over to help Lily.

'What?' asked Gurinder slyly. 'I was just going for the ball . . .'

Lily got up, brushed down her kit and then smiled at me.

'Great goal!' she said.

'Great pass!' I replied.

The next bit of action saw Ant with the ball. He was running towards Parvy, and he tried to nutmeg her. But Parvy is too good for that and she took the ball away. Ant groaned and then stood where he was, not bothering to chase after her.

'COME ON, SON!' shouted Ian. 'Get after her . . .'

Ant groaned again and started jogging back. But he was far too slow. Within seconds Parvy had found Ben, who quickly passed to Pete. Pete skipped past Corky and Emma and then passed to Jason, who was one on one with Gurinder. But Jason didn't shoot either. Instead he played the ball back the way it had come, fooling Abs and Leon, who were both trying to get to the ball. The pass found Lily in space and she slid the ball into the net to make it 2–0.

The practice game went on like that, with our team trying to play like we had been taught and Abs and Ant trying to showboat for the TV crew. At one point Steven and Corky combined to send Abs clear. He raced towards our goal, one on one with Gem. But instead of simply running past her, he tried to do a series of step-overs, just like his favourite Man United player, and fell over. Everyone started laughing, even his new mates. Abs's face grew dark and he started complaining over and over again.

By the time practice was over, we had won the game 6–2 – I scored three goals! – and Abs was livid. He had been trying to be the star, playing up because there was a camera filming us. But it had backfired and after we'd got changed, Ian and Wendy got us all together to talk about how we'd played.

'Not just tonight,' said Ian, 'but on Saturday too, some of us were showing off. Now I know there's a TV crew here, but we must remember the basics, OK? Pass and move. *Simplicity*.'

'Yeah, people,' added Wendy, her American accent getting stronger. 'There ain't no room for stars in this here team . . .'

Most of us nodded.

'We are the Rushton Reds – a team,

y'all . . .' she continued.

Gurinder and Ant sniggered. I looked over at Abs, who was staring at me. I could tell that he was thinking about sniggering too, but he didn't. I shrugged at him – to ask what was up. But he just nodded and looked down.

'Something funny in what we just said?' asked Ian.

'No,' replied Gurinder sullenly.

'OK, then,' said Ian. 'Now get home and remember we've got Evington Eagles away on Saturday. They're third in the league *and* they won the City Cup last year, so it's going to be a tough game. They've beaten every team they've played at home this season.'

'Ian?' asked Dal.

'Yes, Dal?'

'Can we go and visit Steve if we want to?'

Some of the others said they'd like to see him too.

'I'll see what he says,' replied Ian. 'And

ask the hospital. He's very poorly and I'm not sure that the sight of you ugly lot will help him recover,' he joked.

'OK – get going,' added Wendy. 'And remember – TEAM, NOT STARS!'

I looked over at Abs. He was wearing a brand-new Man United top and he had a new haircut. He was also standing right in front of Brian, the cameraman.

'Someone should tell *him* that,' Lily whispered to me.

'He's OK,' I replied. 'I'm sure he'll come round.'

'We'll see,' she said. Then, at the top of her voice, she shouted towards Dal, 'Hubby dearest – are you taking me to see a film?'

The rest of the squad burst into laughter as Dal went red.

'Don't say that!' he told her, for like the millionth time.

It was no use. Lily was mental!

Chapter 8

Saturday

Penny and Parvy were the first team members to get to Evington Eagles' ground. I was right behind them. My dad had to go somewhere and he dropped me off early.

'I thought I'd be the first one here,' I told them.

Penny, who is really slim with short blonde hair which sticks out all over the place, smiled at me.

'We thought we'd get here early and

discuss the way of the football ninja,' she said, acting all mysterious.

'You mean soccer,' corrected Parvy.

'Oh, yes,' replied Penny. 'Although the truest ninja knows that you can use both words and still be right.'

The girls had been going on about football/soccer ninjas since they'd joined the team and I still didn't know what they were talking about.

'What does that *mean*?' I asked.

'Not for you to know,' Parvy told me. 'It's a special thing for girls . . . no boys allowed.'

I grinned at them. 'But we're a *team*, remember?'

'But—' began Penny.

I shook my head. 'No, no, no,' I said. 'That's what Wendy said – no room for stars. So you have to tell me what you're talking about.'

The two girls looked at each other and

then started giggling. Finally, Penny turned to me.

'OK – but we're only going to tell you,' she said. 'And you have to promise never to tell the other *smellies* . . .'

'*Smellies?*' I asked, wondering what she was on about.

'BOYS!' she explained. 'You call us the Barbies and we call you that.'

I frowned. 'But I don't smell,' I protested.

'That's what you think,' replied Parvy. 'You're a boy so you must smell – it's the rules. Boys smell and girls are gorgeous . . .'

'*I* think that's why the cleaners had to use all that bleach on Tuesday,' Penny added. 'To clean up the nasty boy smell!'

I grinned again. Wendy had told my mum the security guard had accidentally knocked over a bucket of bleach, but you couldn't blame Penny for trying to make a point.

'Whatever,' I said. 'Tell me about the ninja thing . . .'

Both of them made a big deal about looking around to make sure that no one could hear them. But we were in the middle of Evington Park and it was huge. There was only one other person about and she was walking a dog. At least I think it was a dog. They were so far away that I couldn't be sure. It could have been a kangaroo for all I knew.

'There's no one here!' I said, getting impatient.

'Oh, all right then,' said Parvy. 'Sister Penny will tell all, but remember the curse . . .'

I groaned. What was she on about now?

'What curse?' I asked.

'Just don't tell anyone,' Parvy explained. 'And then you won't have to find out.'

'Just tell me!'

Penny sat down on the grass and told us to follow suit. The grass was damp and cold.

'It's all about what you do with the ball,' she told me.

'Huh?'

'How you *think* about it and how you *treat* it . . .' she added.

'The *ball*?' I asked.

She nodded. 'Treat the ball well and you will become its friend. And once the ball is your friend, it will do anything for you . . .' she said.

'That's just silly,' I complained. 'Like the ball can become your friend! That's like when my dad got caught by my sister, pretending to be the Tooth Fairy.'

'What happened?' asked Parvy.

'He told Veronica he was just filling in because the Tooth Fairy had the flu. He's as daft as you two are . . .'

'*SSSSHHH!!!!!!!!!!!!!*' whispered Penny.
'Don't let the ball hear you. You'll hurt its
feelings and then it won't like you any
more . . .'

'What *ball*?' I asked, looking around. I
couldn't see any balls.

Parvy pulled a small practice ball from her
bag. It had ARSENAL FC written all over it.

'This ball,' she said.

'But that's a silly little ball,' I told her. 'It's
not a proper ball, is it?'

Parvy and Penny looked at each other,
tut-tutted like my mum does sometimes,
and then shook their heads.

'There *is* only one ball,' explained Penny.

'Huh?'

'Just one – every ball you see is just a
copy of the first ball. The *great* ball . . .'

'You're nuts!' I told them.

'Maybe we are,' replied Parvy. 'But we
know the Way of the Soccer Ninja and you

don't. If you don't believe, you can't know
the magic . . .'

'Crazy,' I said.

'Trust the ball, let it be your friend and the
game is yours,' said Penny.

'Love the ball, treat it with respect,' added
Parvy.

'Bonkers!' I complained.

'Do you want to know or not?' asked
Penny, sternly like a teacher.

I nodded.

'OK then – so shut up and pay attention.'

She stood up and Parvy threw the practice
ball at her. Penny took it on her left foot and
did ten keep-ups with it.

'Your turn,' she said to me.

'That's simple,' I replied, standing up.

Penny threw the ball at me and I managed
two keep-ups before I lost control.

'That's not fair!' I moaned. 'You didn't
throw it to me properly.'

Parvy giggled. 'Fair's got nothing to do with it. You aren't fluent in the Way of the Ninja . . . the ball is not your friend . . .'

I laughed. 'So what about at the last training session when I scored a hat trick?' I asked.

'That was just easy stuff,' Penny told me. '*Anyone* can do that. The soccer ninja can do *more* than that though. Being a ninja is like being *super*-good – not just good.'

I scratched my head. 'Throw me the ball again,' I challenged. 'This time I'll do more than you did.'

Penny got the ball and threw it to me. But this time I didn't even manage two keep-ups.

'Fix!' I groaned. 'There's something wrong with the ball!'

Parvy snorted. 'That's your first mistake,' she told me. 'A proper soccer ninja never, *ever*, says that. It's *never* the ball – it's always the *player* who does it wrong. That's rule number one.'

I groaned again and started praying that the rest of the team would hurry up.

'Rule number two,' said Penny. 'The ball must never be shouted at or told off. Love the ball and the ball will be your servant.'

'Weirdos!' I said childishly, whilst making a swirling motion with my finger at my left temple.

'Rule number three,' added Parvy. 'The soccer ninja will never be perfect. She must keep on practising, every day, and never believe that she has become the best. Because she can always, *always* become better still!'

'Number four,' said Penny, as I thought about running away, screaming. They really were completely crazy. I began to wish that I hadn't asked. 'Rule four tells us that the true soccer ninja must love simplicity. Never,

ever, *ever* forget that soccer is about passing the ball. Let the ball do the work and glory will be yours . . .'

I stopped them before they could continue. Some of the other players were coming towards us.

'The rest of the team is here,' I told them.

'That's a shame,' said Penny. 'We were going to tell you some more of the rules.'

'How many are there?' I asked.

'At least fifty,' explained Parvy. 'You can't know them all. You learn them as you become a better ninja . . .'

'Nutters!' I said, doing the swirling thing with my finger again.

Parvy whispered, 'I'll come up to you in the game and tell you when the Barbies have called on the ninja skills – then you can see for yourself.'

'Huh?'

'Just wait and see,' she said, winking at me, just as Dal arrived.

'Hey, Chris,' he said.

'Hey, Dal.'

'Are you OK?' he asked me.

'I am now,' I replied. 'Now that those two crazy girls have gone . . .'

Dal shrugged. 'They're OK,' he told me. 'It's Lily who's mad.'

Lily must have heard her name because she appeared like a ghost. She pinched Dal's cheek and then whispered something to me.

'Never tell,' she said.

My eyes nearly popped out of my head. Lily hadn't heard me speaking to Parvy and Penny and she'd only just arrived so I was sure that she hadn't spoken to her friends. How could she know what they'd just said to me?

'But—' I stuttered.

'The soccer ninja always knows . . .' she said mysteriously before going back to teasing Dal.

I shook my head in confusion. I was having one weird morning.

Chapter 9

It got stranger too. Once we were all there, Wendy and Ian got us together. Abs was still ignoring us, but I couldn't see Ant or Gurinder anywhere. They were late.

'We have some news for you,' Ian told us. 'We've noticed recently that there has been a split in the team. It's not serious but we have seen it. Well, on Thursday night we decided to let one of the squad go. That player is Gurinder. There are reasons for it, but we won't go into those. Suffice to say that he wasn't ready to give his all for the Reds or to be a full team member . . .'

Wendy cleared her throat. 'And then this morning we found out that Ant has gone too,' she said. 'Both he and Gurinder have gone to play for Langton Blues.'

'NAH!' shouted Byron. 'That's just wrong, man! Traitors . . .'

'Calm down, son,' replied Ian. 'If they're not playing for us, they can go where they wish. We just need to focus on our team.'

'Now,' continued Wendy, 'we are obviously going to need some new players. Corky's sister is coming along to the next practice and hopefully one or two more of my old team will join up. But if you do know of any other players, boys or girls, let us know at the end of today's game . . .'

I waited for the familiar sound of Abs moaning about yet another girl playing. But when I glanced over at him, he looked shocked and he kept really quiet.

Lily whispered in my ear. 'His new friends have deserted him,' she said.

I nodded. 'It's a good job he's still got his *real* friends here,' I replied.

Lily smiled at me. 'You're really cool, you are,' she told me. 'After everything he's done, you still want to be his friend.'

'He *is* still my friend,' I said. 'And he's still a *Red* . . .'

Lily nodded. I glanced over at Abs again and this time he saw me. His expression was downcast and he looked a bit lost.
I smiled broadly and stuck my thumb up.
He looked even more shocked. And then he kind of smiled back a little. But he still didn't speak.

'OK, people,' said Wendy. 'Let's get out there, and remember what we talked about on Thursday – *team* players, not *stars*! Just ignore the TV crew – please.'

'YEAH!!!!!!!!!!!!!!!!!!!!!' the whole squad shouted.

'We are one win away from going third in the league,' Ian reminded us. 'Beat the Eagles and we go above them. That's all the motivation you need . . . now get out there!'

'FOR STEVE!' shouted Ben.

'STEVE!!!!!!!!!!!!!!!!!!!!!!!!!!!' we all replied.

I ran onto the pitch with Abs by my side.

'Easy,' I said to him.

'Easy,' he replied, letting me know that things were fine again.

The team that Ian and Wendy picked was the same as the one that started against Streetly Celtic. Lily was on the bench again but she didn't complain. Instead she went round to each of the starting eleven and told them to play their socks off.

'If we go up to third, we'll show them that we're a proper team,' she told us all.

We took up our positions and faced the Evington Eagles. From the moment they saw us, the Eagles had been taunting us. One in particular – a big, burly lad called Adam who had been at our trials but gone to Evington instead – looked very threatening too. We had history with him! But we were so used to the insults that we mostly just ignored them. Instead, as I looked around at the team, I could see that everyone was really determined.

We won the coin toss and chose to kick off. I took the ball from the referee and placed it on the centre circle.

Abs joined me.

'You OK?' I asked him.

'Yeah,' he replied. 'Let's show these fools how to play the game properly. Especially that big lump, Adam!'

Within minutes of the start we were on the attack. Leon had won a free kick on the right and Ben went across to take it. Ian urged Steven and Jason to make their way into the box. I was standing just outside it, with an Eagles player holding onto my shirt.

'Let go!' I shouted.

The lad smirked at me and told me to get lost. But then he moved away, thinking that Ben would put a cross into the box. Only he didn't. He played the ball square to Byron, who sent it on to Corky. Corky ran right at the heart of the Eagles' defence. Just as he was about to be tackled, he passed to Abs, who let a fierce drive go. But the Eagles' keeper saw it coming and got his hands to it.

'Nice try,' I told my friend.

Abs shrugged. 'There was no one else to pass to,' he said, as though he was ashamed of shooting.

I didn't say anything and ran back to my position. Over on the touchline I saw Hayley interviewing Lily and I wondered what they were talking about. Then the ball sailed over my head and the Eagles were on the attack. They were a big team with lots of tall players. The ball ended up with their winger, a black-haired lad called Milorad. He played the ball into the box, but Dal won it.

I thought he would clear the ball, but he didn't just whack it. Instead he saw that Byron was free and passed to him. Byron turned to face the Eagles' goal and ran with the ball. Three of their players tried to get to him, but Byron is a really strong runner and he rode all of their challenges before finding Corky out on the left wing. Corky stopped the ball, looked up and saw that Byron had continued his run, into the box.

I saw my chance! I ran alongside Byron and then moved to my right. Both central defenders went towards Byron. Corky waited and then passed the ball to me. I controlled the ball with my right foot,

pushing it forward and then hit it. The ball flew past their keeper.

1–0!

'*YESSSSSSSSSSSSSS!!!!!!!!!!!!!!!!!!!!!!!!*'
I yelled, setting off to celebrate. I didn't know what to do so I ran for the touchline and jumped on Ian, who looked really embarrassed. The rest of the team joined in until the referee told us to calm down. But we were *winning* against one of the top three teams in our league. There was no way we were going to stay calm!

From the restart we put the Eagles under more pressure. Byron, Abs and Corky all went close to scoring. And then Parvy ran all the way out of defence, taking the ball past three of their players – *including* Adam – and saw her wicked shot hit the post. We were all over them and feeling really confident. But with five minutes left in the half, the Eagles went and equalized.

It started with a rubbish pass from me, so I felt really bad about it. I was facing my own goal and instead of looking round to see who was there, I stopped concentrating. I tried to pass to Dal, who was to my left, but the ball didn't reach him and their winger, Milorad, sneaked in and took it. He crossed for a really tall lad called Will, who smashed it home.

1–1!

Chapter 10

At half-time Ian gathered us all together whilst Wendy handed out slices of orange. He told us that we were doing really well.

'Move as a unit,' he told us. 'If you pass the ball, try and move into a space after-wards. That way you can always get the ball back. Play in little triangles like Steve showed you during our first training session together. Move up and down the pitch like that. Triangles . . .'

Corky put up his hand.

'Yes, son?' asked Ian.

'My leg hurts,' said Corky. 'I think I twisted my knee.'

Ian looked at Wendy.

'OK!' she said cheerfully. 'Corky, take a rest. Penny, get ready to go on in his place.'

Ian talked to us some more and then we gathered together in a huddle.

Wendy told us to concentrate. 'Play as a team, y'all!' she said. Her voice was encouraging and I forgot about the mistake I'd made for their equalizer.

'COME ON, YOU REDS!' shouted Byron.

'YEAH!!!!!!!!' we all yelled back.

The second half kicked off with another attack from the Eagles. They were bearing down on our goal and I could see that Steven and Dal were outnumbered. I sprinted back to help out but it was too late. Their strikers played a one-two with each other and Will scored again.

It was 2–1 . . .

'COME ON!' urged Wendy. 'Let's keep those heads up.'

We restarted and tried to get forward, but the Eagles had us pinned back. They were a really good team and we were getting outplayed.

But then Ian swapped Ben for Lily and things changed. Lily stayed out on the left wing, with Penny on the right. That meant that their defenders had to stay with them. This left us lots more room in the middle and we started to play again. Slowly but surely we began to get stronger. And nobody – not even Abs – was glancing over at the sidelines where the TV people were follow-ing the action.

Byron and Jason were playing out of their skins. They were beginning to run the show in midfield and the Eagles players were looking tired. Adam was puffing away like mad. He might have been big, but he certainly wasn't fit! Jason and Corky both outran him several times and he was looking more and more fed up. Good! Shows he picked the wrong team . . .

Then Jason won the ball in the centre with a fierce tackle and played the ball out to Lily. Lily stopped it and waited for her defender to challenge for the ball. When he did, she lifted it over his leg and sprinted down the left wing. At the by-line she sent a great cross into the box.

Abs was charging in and he managed to get his toe to the ball just before the Eagles' keeper could reach it. The ball arced over the keeper and into the net to make it 2–2!

'GOALLLLLLLLLLLLLLLLL!!!!!!!!!!!!!!!!!!!!!!!!!!!' screamed Abs, running straight into Jason and Byron. He was really happy and when he saw Jason, he jumped on him.

Lily trotted over to me and smiled. 'Back to normal, then?' she asked.

'It looks like it,' I told her.

Parvy came over and tapped me on the shoulder. 'It's time,' she told me.

'Huh?'

'For the sacred ninja skills,' she explained.

I grinned. 'Go on then,' I said, challenging her. 'You and the rest of the Barbies show me what you've got . . .'

Parvy smiled back. 'Keep watching,' she boasted.

Five minutes later Parvy was defending an Eagles attack. The attacker was quick and strong and he looked like he would go past her. But Parvy waited and, at just the right moment, she nicked the ball away. Another Eagles player was closer to it than she was, but she didn't give up. She ran to the ball and then spun round in a pirouette, taking the ball away from the attacker.

I had to shake my head. I'd never seen anyone do that, ever! It was well impressive. Next, Parvy passed to Penny, who ran down the right wing with the ball. When her defender came in, she skipped past him, towards the corner of their box. She had two more defenders on her case, but she just ignored them. She moved the ball from her left foot to her right and curled in a shot.

The ball seemed to swerve in mid-air and then it clipped the underside of the cross-bar. It flew off the bar, into the net.

3–2!

This time we all ran towards the scorer, but it was Abs who was first to reach her. He nearly picked her up off the ground, he was so happy.

'COME ON, YOU GIRLS!!!!!!!!!!!!' he shouted.

Me, Dal, Jason and Byron looked at each other in amazement.

Lily joined in. 'Did he really just say what I thought he said?' she asked. 'And in front of the telly people too!'

'Yep!' I replied, feeling really proud of Abs.

I turned to retake my position and saw Parvy beaming a smile at me.

'Did you see it?' she asked.

I nodded.

'See?' she added. 'Never question the power of the ninja.'

I laughed. 'Bet you can't do it again,' I said.

But she could. In fact she went one better. Two minutes before the end, Jason was fouled about twenty yards from goal. When the free kick was given, Parvy took the ball from Abs, who had grabbed it first. I thought Abs would complain but he didn't.

'Trust me,' Parvy said to him. He nodded and said OK.

As she placed the ball, I went over to see what she would do.

'You have to believe in the ball,' she said mysteriously.

'What does that mean?' I asked.

She grinned. 'It means that you don't always have to look at the ball to know where it is, and where it's going,' she replied.

I watched in amazement as she ran towards the ball. At the last moment, instead of looking at the ball, Parvy turned her head towards me. There was no way on earth she'd be able to score like that. I watched the ball, feeling sure that it would sail over the bar or go hopelessly wide. But I was wrong. The ball whizzed and zipped and dipped its way into the top corner of the goal.

It was 4–2!

There was no way we would lose now. Third place was ours.

Parvy didn't celebrate. Instead she turned to me. 'Do you want to be a soccer ninja now, smelly?' she asked.

'That was just . . . MAGIC!' I replied.

'Told you!' she added.

At the final whistle, Abs came over and put his arm round me.

'Are we friends again?' I asked.

'Yes,' he replied. 'I'm sorry about the last few days . . . honest.'

I smiled. 'Forget about it,' I said.

Abs said OK, and then he walked over to Lily and the rest of the Barbies.

'I'm sorry that I didn't want you in the team,' he said to them.

Dal and Jason came up and watched too.

'He's gone mad,' said Jason.

'Nah,' replied Dal, 'he's nearly normal now.'

I watched as Lily thanked him.

Abs told her it was fine. 'I thought you'd all be rubbish,' he admitted. 'But you lot are stars . . . proper STARS!'

We had just beaten one of the best teams in the league and gone third in the table.

And Abs had finally accepted that the Rushton Reds were a special team.

All we needed now was for Steve to get better. And to beat Langton Blues – including Gurinder and Ant – in the Cup. That was our next game, and I could hardly wait!

'COME ON, YOU REDS!!!!' I sang as I walked off the pitch.

ABOUT THE AUTHOR

Bali Rai thinks he is a very lucky man. He gets to write all day if he wants to, or go into schools to speak to his readers about what they think of his books. He loves films, music, reading, seeing friends and watching his beloved Liverpool FC.

Bali played for his school team as a defender and loved it. He has been a lifelong football fan since he began watching *Match of the Day* at the age of four with his dad. He enjoys talking and arguing about Liverpool FC, and would like to be Rafa Benitez's or Steven Gerrard's personal servant, but if this does not happen he is happy to carry on writing for his thousands of fans.

Bali was very honoured that his short novel *Dream On* (about a young footballer) was chosen for the first Booked-Up list and was made available to every Year 7 school child.

Bali 's books are now in ten languages and he gets to travel all over the world to meet his readers. He hopes that he can encourage anyone to have a go at writing and to find a love of reading. He has won lots of book awards and really enjoys winning the ones that are voted for by the real readers – you!

Bali lives in his home city of Leicester . He has a lovely new wife and a football-crazy daughter.

Don't miss any of the titles in this action-packed football series from an author with real street cred!

Available now:

Bali Rai

STARTING ELEVEN
MISSING!

And coming soon . . .
GLORY!